I0813888

Seasons and You

SPRING

By Shalini Vallepur

KidHaven PUBLISHING

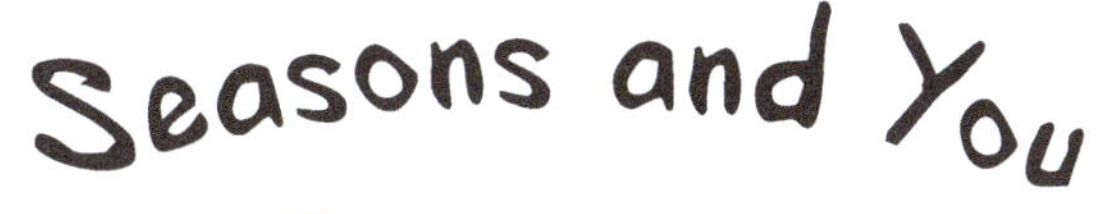

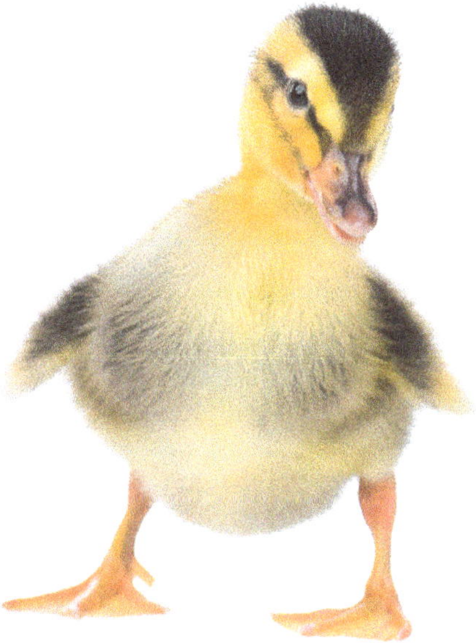

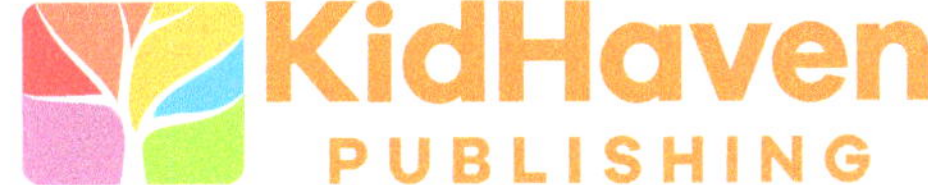

Published in 2023 by **KidHaven Publishing, an Imprint of Greenhaven Publishing, LLC**
29 East 21st Street
New York, NY 10010

Edited by: John Wood

Designed by: Danielle Webster-Jones

Cataloging-in-Publication Data

Names: Vallepur, Shalini.
Title: Spring / Shalini Vallepur.
Description: New York : KidHaven Publishing, 2023. | Series: Seasons and you | Includes glossary and index.
Identifiers: ISBN 9781534541337 (pbk.) | ISBN 9781534541351 (library bound) | ISBN 9781534541344 (6 pack) | ISBN 9781534541368 (ebook)
Subjects: LCSH: Spring--Juvenile literature.
Classification: LCC QB637.5 V35 2023 | DDC 508.2--dc23

Manufactured in the United States of America

CPSIA compliance information: Batch #CSKH23: For further information contact Greenhaven Publishing LLC, New York, New York at 1-844-317-7404.

Please visit our website, www.greenhavenpublishing.com. For a free color catalog of all our high-quality books, call toll free 1-844-317-7404 or fax 1-844-317-7405.

Find us on

IMAGE CREDITS

All images are courtesy of Shutterstock.com, unless otherwise specified. With thanks to Getty Images, Thinkstock Photo and iStockphoto. Cover & throughout – TY Lim, ElenVD, Bozena Fulawka, Anna Nefedova, Tainar, Irina Barilo, Alexander Mak, PAKULA PIOTR, Delpixel, Diana Taliun, DenisNata, Erik Lam, Oliver Hoffmann, Soru Epotok, Yellow Cat, Ioan Panaite, Nattika, Olena Zaskochenko, Dmitry Zimin, Cozy nook, JIANG HONGYAN, irin-k, MRS. SUCHARUT CHOUNYOO, rob, pukach, Anton-Burakov, Bozena Fulawka. 4 – LightField Studios. 5 – Volodymyr Burdiak. 6 – imtmphoto. 7 – Shark_749. 8 – Varina C. 9 – Romrodphoto. 10 – Aksenova Natalya. 11 – Dave Massey. 12 – Ad Oculos. 13 – oksana2010, KrimKate, Lepas. 14 – Marina Yesina. 15 – vagabond54. 16 – Rita_Kochmarjova. 17 – Sonsedska Yuliia. 18 – StockImageFactory.com, Kitsana1980. 19 – picture cells. 20 – Life Junkie Studio. 21 – AppleEyesStudio. 22–23 – Honza Krej.

CONTENTS

Words that look like this can be found in the glossary on page 24.

SPRING!

Welcome to spring! Spring is a season. Most places in the world have four seasons. Each one has different weather.

Spring, summer, autumn, and winter are the four seasons.

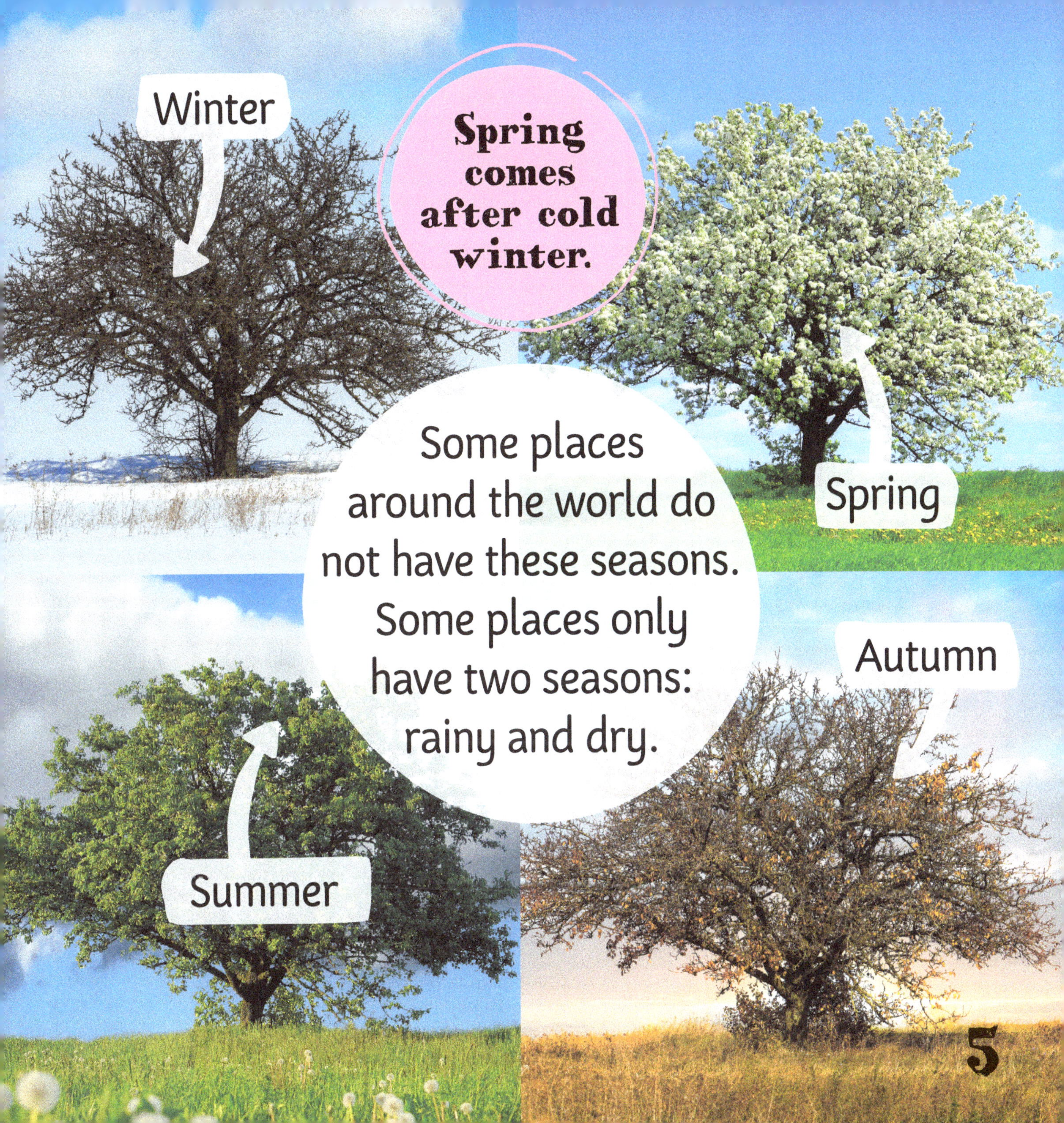

Spring comes after cold winter.

Some places around the world do not have these seasons. Some places only have two seasons: rainy and dry.

SPRING WEATHER

It usually gets warmer in spring and the days begin to get longer. There may be lots of sunshine during spring.

Spring can also be quite rainy! The rain helps plants and flowers to grow. Sometimes there is very light rain and sometimes there are heavy showers.

SPLISH SPLASH!

Even though the sun is out in spring, it may still be cold! You might need to wear a sweater and jacket to stay warm.

Raincoats and rain boots will keep you dry when it is rainy and wet outside. You could bring an umbrella too.

PLANTS IN SPRING

When there is lots of sunshine and rain, plants start to grow. Many trees grow back the leaves that they lost in winter.

These are buds. Buds grow into leaves or flowers.

Some flowers blossom during spring. Butterflies and bees go from flower to flower to find nectar, which they like to eat.

Have you ever seen a butterfly or bee on a flower?

Some fruits and vegetables are in season in spring. This means that they are ready to be harvested and eaten.
This rhubarb is almost ready to eat!

Lots of different fruits and vegetables are harvested during spring around the world. Here are a few!

ANIMALS IN SPRING

Many animals hibernate in winter when it is too cold. They come out of hibernation in spring when it gets warmer.

Groundhogs hibernate inside burrows.

Poorwill birds hibernate over winter. They come out again during spring when there are more bugs to eat. While hibernating, they can go months without eating.

Baby rabbits are often born in spring.

Many animals are born during spring. Spring is the perfect time for baby animals. There is warmer weather and lots of food.

Lots of farm animals are born during spring too. How many animals can you name?

Baby rabbits are called kittens.

TIME TO CELEBRATE!

During spring, there are lots of festivals around the world. Holi is a colorful Hindu festival that comes from India.

People build bonfires and throw colorful powder.

Sakura trees usually blossom during spring in Japan. People visit the sakura trees during festivals called hanami.

Millions of tulips bloom in Ottawa, Canada, every spring. People travel to see the beautiful tulips. It is the biggest tulip festival in the world.

Songkran is a Buddhist festival that takes place in spring. People splash water at each other to welcome the new year.

Do you celebrate any festivals during spring?

THE END OF SPRING

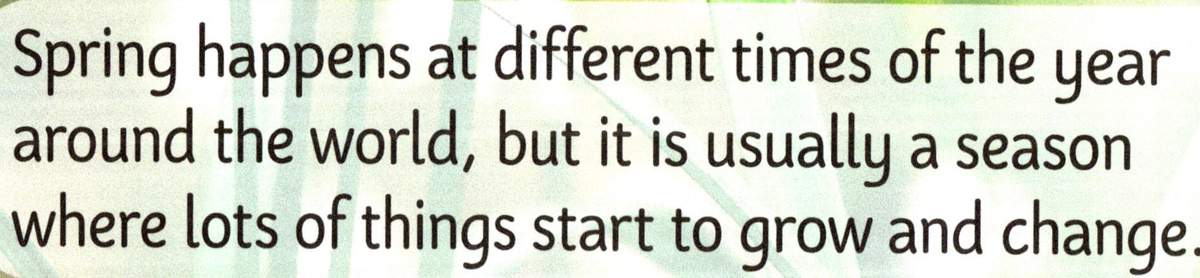

Spring happens at different times of the year around the world, but it is usually a season where lots of things start to grow and change.

As spring passes, the days keep getting warmer and longer. Animals are born and flowers bloom. It isn't long before summer arrives!

What's your favorite thing about spring?

GLOSSARY

blossom to make or grow flowers

Buddhist having to do with Buddhism, a religion that follows the teachings of Buddha

burrows holes or tunnels dug by an animal

celebrate to do something special for an important event

festivals special times of the year when people come together to remember or do something

harvested when fully grown crops have been picked

hibernate to sleep or rest during winter

Hindu having to do with Hinduism, one of the oldest religions in the world, which started in India

in season when a plant grows best

INDEX